WHO WILL YOU MEET ON SANTA CLAUS STREET?

To Noah and the Unicorn that started this all.
G.P.

To Julia, Happy Christmas x
T.B.

SIMON & SCHUSTER
First published in Great Britain in 2021 by Simon & Schuster UK Ltd
1st Floor, 222 Gray's Inn Road, London, WC1X 8HB
Text copyright © 2021 Gareth Peter • Illustrations copyright © 2021 Tim Budgen
The right of Gareth Peter and Tim Budgen to be identified as the author and illustrator
of this work has been asserted by them in accordance with the Copyright,
Designs and Patents Act, 1988 • All rights reserved, including
the right of reproduction in whole or in part in any form
A CIP catalogue record for this book is available
from the British Library upon request
ISBNs: 978-1-4711-9939-4 (PB) 978-1-4711-9940-0 (eB)
Printed in China
1 3 5 7 9 10 8 6 4 2

WHO WILL YOU MEET ON SANTA CLAUS STREET?

GARETH PETER • TIM BUDGEN

SIMON & SCHUSTER
London New York Sydney Toronto New Delhi

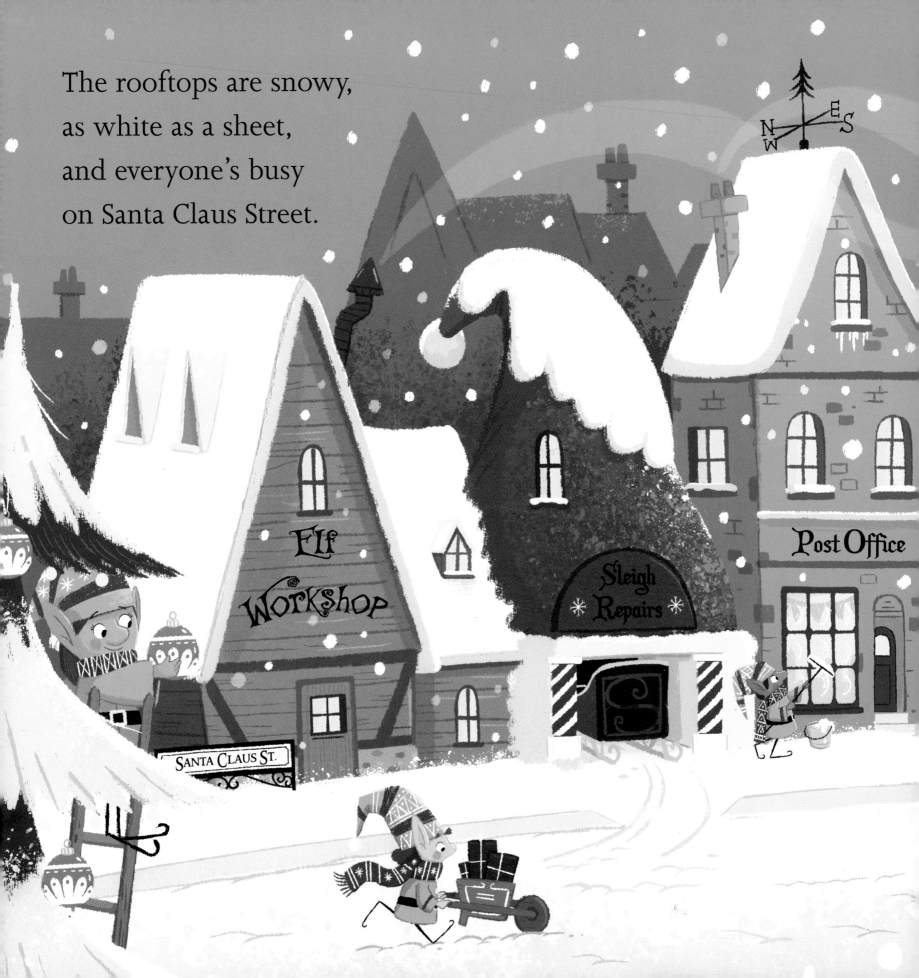

The rooftops are snowy,
as white as a sheet,
and everyone's busy
on Santa Claus Street.

Elf Workshop

Sleigh Repairs

Post Office

SANTA CLAUS ST.

You see, all of the elves have a challenge today:
to gather the presents and load up the sleigh.

Cinnamon

Pet Shop

Let's say Merry Christmas to . . .

Wrapping Elf.

Flapping Elf.

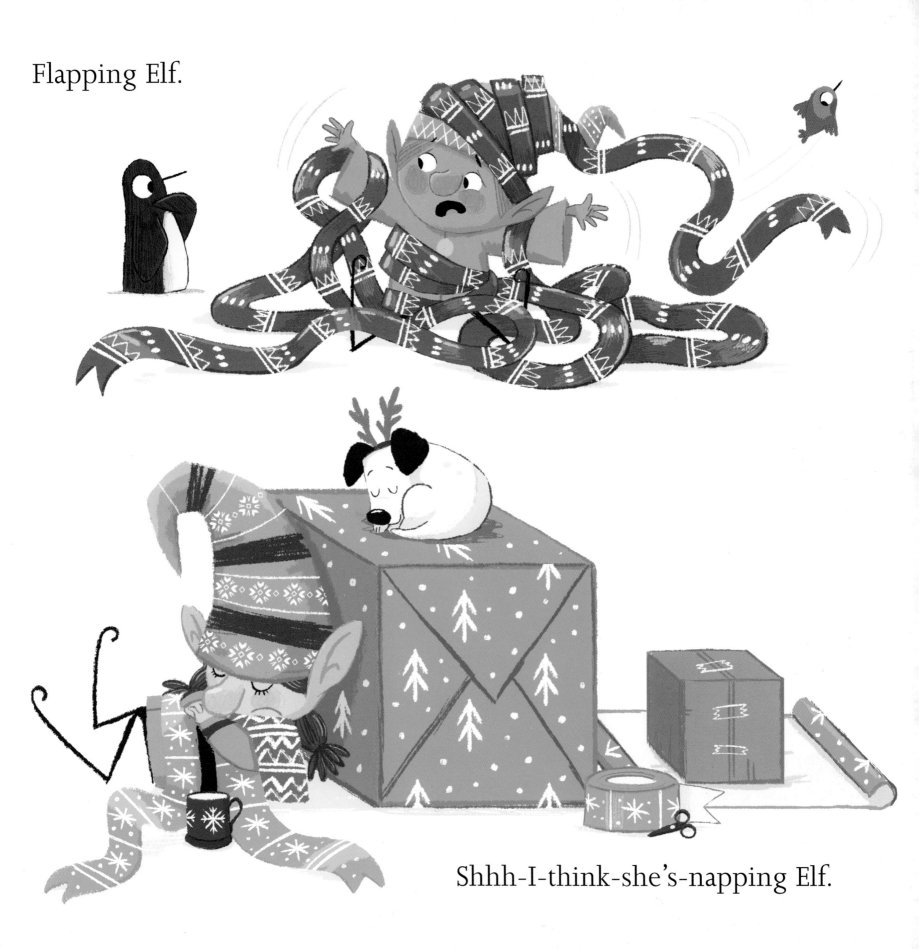

Shhh-I-think-she's-napping Elf.

Picky Elf.

Licky Elf.

Getting-very-sticky Elf.

Hairy Elf.

Elf Esteem

Scary Elf.

Sparkly-treetop-fairy Elf.

Reading Elf.

Feeding Elf.

Carol-sing-song-leading Elf.

Sneaky Elf.

Cheeky Elf.

Looks-a-little-peaky Elf.

Handy Elf.

Candy Elf.

Dreams-of-sun-and-sandy Elf.

Weeping Elf.

Employee of the Week

Sweeping Elf.

Creeping, peeping, leaping Elf.

Twisting Elf.

Listing Elf.

Very-stressed-assisting Elf.

Sewing Elf.

Glowing Elf.

Shouldn't-you-be-going Elf . . .

. . . as Santa's here! The sleigh is full.
It's nearly time to fly.

And now the reindeer have arrived,
we have to say goodbye.

But first, let's double check the list – whoops!
One more Elf to meet.
Say Ho, Ho, Ho, to . . .

...YoursELF.

Welcome to our street!

Look out for more hilarious books in the
Who Will You Meet? series!
(And did you spot the dinosaur character in THIS book?!)

Who Will You Meet on Dinosaur Street?
coming soon . . .